Dear Parents,

This is a Stepping Stone Book™ by the Berenstains. We have drawn on decades of experience creating books for children to make these books not only easy to read but also exciting, suspenseful, and meaningful enough to be read over and over again. Our chapter books will include mysteries, life lessons, action and adventure tales, and laugh-out-loud stories. They are written in short sentences and simple language that will take your youngsters happily past beginning readers and into the exciting world of chapter books they can read all by themselves!

Happy reading!

The Berenstains

BOOKS IN THIS SERIES:

The Goofy, Goony Guy

The Haunted Lighthouse

The Runamuck Dog Show

The Wrong Crowd

www.randomhouse.com/kids
www.berenstainbears.com

Library of Congress Cataloging-in-Publication Data
Berenstain, Stan, 1923–
The runamuck dog show / by Stan & Jan Berenstain.
  p. cm.
(A stepping stone book)
SUMMARY: Brother and Sister Bear and their cousin, Fred, plan a dog show for the
annual church fair that has everyone in Beartown excited, including Too-Tall and
his gang, who have a plan for stirring things up.
ISBN 0-375-81271-7 (trade) — ISBN 0-375-91271-1 (lib. bdg.)
[1. Dog shows—Fiction. 2. Fairs—Fiction. 3. Bears—Fiction. 4. Dogs—Fiction.]
I. Berenstain, Jan, 1923– . II. Title.
PZ7.B4483 Ru 2001 [Fic]—dc21 00-064079

Printed in the United States of America July 2001
10 9 8 7 6 5 4 3 2 1

The Runamuck Dog Show

The Berenstains

A STEPPING STONE BOOK™

Random House New York

The Bear family usually did things together Saturday morning. But not *this* Saturday.

Brother and Sister were sitting on the front steps.

Mama hadn't said beans to them since breakfast.

Neither had Papa.

They were much too busy getting ready for the church fair.

Mama was in charge of the bake

sale. She'd been baking cakes and pies all day.

Not that Brother and Sister didn't like cakes and pies.

They *loved* cakes and pies.

But they wouldn't get any of the church-fair goodies. They could just hear Mama if they tried:

"Brother Bear, get your finger out of that icing! That cake is for the church fair!"

Or:

"Sister Bear, let that pie alone! It's for the church fair!"

It was the same with Papa.

He was in charge of building things for the church fair. He was building tables for all the sales.

The cubs liked to spend time in Papa's shop. They liked to watch him work. They liked to help. They liked to bring him tools.

But not today.

"Please, cubs," he said. "I don't want to be rude. But the church fair is next Saturday. That's just a week away. I have work to do. I can't have you underfoot."

So they sat on the front steps and felt sorry for themselves.

They could hear the phone ringing inside. But it wasn't ringing for them. It was ringing for Mama.

The sounds of hammering and

sawing were coming from Papa's shop. Those sounds were usually music to their ears.

But not today.

Today they just made Brother and Sister feel left out.

The church fair was a big deal in Beartown.

It was held every year.

It had always been pretty much a grown-up thing.

Mama and Papa weren't trying to be mean.

It was just that the church fair was such a big job. And there was so little time.

"I have an idea," said Brother.

"Let's go over to Cousin Fred's."

"What for?" said Sister. "It'll be the same over there. Fred's mom is busy with the church fair, too. She's in charge of the clothing sale."

"At least it's something to do," said Brother. "Maybe we can take Snuff for a walk."

Fred was their cousin. His house was close by. Snuff was Fred's dog. He liked to go back and forth. He was almost as much Brother and Sister's dog as he was Fred's.

Cousin Fred was sitting on his front steps. Snuff was sitting beside him. When Snuff saw Brother and

6

Sister, he came running. He was glad to see them. He barked. He jumped all over them. He had something in his mouth.

It was his leash.

"Hello, Fred," said Brother. "What's happening?"

"What's happening is the church fair," said Fred. "My mom is in charge of the clothing sale. Folks have been bringing old clothes here all morning. My house looks like an old-clothes store."

"It's the same at our house," said Brother. "At our house it's the bake sale and building tables."

"Fred, I think Snuff wants to go for a walk," said Sister. "What do you say?"

"I say fine," said Fred. "Where do you want to walk?"

"How about downtown?" said Brother.

"Okay with me," said Fred. He snapped on Snuff's leash. They headed downtown.

Downtown was busy on Saturday morning.

Folks were shopping.

They were doing business.

They were just walking around.

Fred, Brother, and Sister walked Snuff along Main Street.

They walked past the library. Mrs. Stacks was on the steps.

"Good morning, cubs," said Mrs. Stacks.

"Good morning, Mrs. Stacks," said the cubs.

"Arf!" said Snuff.

They walked past the police station. Chief Bruno was coming out.

"Good morning, cubs," said Chief Bruno.

"Good morning, Chief Bruno," said the cubs.

"Arf!" said Snuff.

Chief Bruno's daughter was Babs Bruno. She was a friend. She had a dog named Butch.

They walked past the church. There was a big sign on the gate. It said:

```
┌─────────────────────────────────┐
│                                   │
│         COMING SOON:              │
│         THE ANNUAL                │
│         CHURCH FAIR               │
│                                   │
│     TIME: NEXT SATURDAY           │
│     PLACE: THE CHURCHYARD         │
│                                   │
└─────────────────────────────────┘
```

Minister Jones was standing beside the sign. He was in charge of the church fair.

"Good morning, cubs," said Minister Jones.

"Good morning, Minister Jones," said the cubs.

"Arf!" said Snuff.

"Will you be coming to the fair?" asked Minister Jones.

"I guess so," said Brother. "Our mom is in charge of the bake sale."

"And our dad is making the tables," said Sister.

"My mom is in charge of the clothing sale," said Fred.

Minister Jones had a list. He looked at it.

"Yes, that's so," he said. "And Lizzy Bruin's mother is in charge of the attic sale."

Lizzy was another friend. She had a dog named Taffy.

"Will there be anything new?" asked Sister.

Minister Jones looked at his list.

"No," he said. "It looks like the same old same old. The fair will be the same as last year."

"Oh," said Brother.

"But I would like some new ideas. Something for cubs," said the minister. "I'd like that very much.

Do you have any ideas?"

"We could think about it," said Brother. "What do you say, gang? Should we think about it?"

"I think we should," said Fred.

As they walked along, they thought about it.

"How about an old-toy sale?" said Fred.

"I don't know," said Brother. "They're already having three sales."

"Not only that," said Sister, "I love my old toys. I wouldn't give them up."

"Neither would I," said Fred.

"That makes three of us," said Brother.

All around them they saw folks they knew. Some of them were walking their dogs.

They were still thinking of ideas.

"How about if we put on a play?" said Brother. "One of the plays we did at school."

"I don't know," said Fred. "Everybody has already seen those plays."

"Besides," said Sister, "you have to pay to get into the fair. Who would pay to see us in a play?"

"Sister's got a point," said Brother.

The supermarket was busy on Saturday morning.

They saw Sam McNab coming out of the supermarket. He was another friend. He had a dog, too. It was a big sheepdog named Cuddles. Sam was carrying a big bag.

"Hi, Sam," said Brother. "What are you doing downtown?"

"We ran out of dog food for Cuddles," said Sam. "I have to hurry home and feed him."

They were still trying to think of ideas for the fair.

"How about this?" said Sister. "How about a spelling bee?"

"A spelling bee?" said Brother.

"You've got to be kidding!" said Fred.

"I guess I am," said Sister.

"Look!" said Brother. "There's Greeves, Lady Grizzly's butler, with Yasha and Sasha, her two wolfhounds!"

Yasha and Sasha were huge. They pulled Greeves along as if he were on wheels.

Snuff got excited when he saw them.

"Arf! Arf!" he said.

The wolfhounds snubbed Snuff.

Brother sighed.

"I guess we're out of ideas," he said.

"I guess so," said Fred.

But Sister wasn't out of ideas.

One was forming in her head.

Dogs, she thought.

Sometimes ideas are catching.

Brother was thinking the same thing.

Dogs, he thought.

So was Cousin Fred.

Dogs, he thought.

They had a dog. Most of their friends had dogs. There were more dogs in Beartown than you could shake a stick at.

Fred looked at Sister.

Sister looked at Brother.

They all looked at Snuff.

Then with one voice, they said, "LET'S HAVE A DOG SHOW AT THE FAIR!"

They clapped each other on the back.

"Awesome!" they shouted.

"Arf!" said Snuff.

"Come on," said Sister. "Let's go back and tell Minister Jones."

"Wait," said Fred. "Look across the street."

It was the Too-Tall gang. They were being chased out of the dime store.

They were up to no good.

The cubs knew them all too well.

"I wonder what they did," said Sister.

"With the Too-Tall gang, you never know," said Brother. "Come on, let's tell Minister Jones our idea."

"I like it," said Minister Jones after they had told him. "I like the idea of a dog show very much. Until now, the fair has been mostly for grownups. This will be something for cubs. But there's not much time. How will we get the word out?"

"We could make posters," said Brother.

"Good thinking," said Minister Jones. "We can print them on the church computer."

"We'll post them all over town," said Fred.

"And we can tell our friends," said Sister. "Most of our friends have dogs."

"What about prizes?" asked Brother.

"You can't have a dog show without prizes," said Sister.

"Mr. Brown is a member of the church," said Minister Jones. "His company makes dog food. I'll ask him for the prizes."

"We'll need a judge," said Fred.

"How about Dr. Hairball, the vet?" said Minister Jones.

"Perfect," said Sister.

"And we'll need a stage to show the dogs on," said Fred.

"Our dad can build one," said Sister.

They told Mama and Papa all about it when they got home.

"A dog show, you say?" said Papa.

"That's right," said Brother. "We planned it all out with Minister Jones. The show will begin with a grand parade of dogs. Then each dog will do a trick."

"We're putting posters up all

over town. We're calling all our friends," said Sister.

"Well, what do you think?" asked Brother.

Papa said it sounded great.

Mama wasn't so sure.

Soon dogs and dog owners all over town were getting ready for the dog show.

The next day, Brother and Sister went over to Fred's. He was working with Snuff. They were getting ready for the show. Snuff got excited when he saw them. He gave them each a big, wet kiss.

"Down, Snuff!" said Brother.

"That tickles!" said Sister.

"Skip the kisses, Snuff," said Fred. "We have work to do."

Snuff sat at Fred's feet.

"Snuff, shake hands!" said Fred.

Snuff rolled over.

"Snuff, roll over!" said Fred.

Snuff stood up.

"Snuff, sit up and beg!" said Fred.

Snuff played dead.

"Hmm," said Brother. "I think you've got your work cut out for you."

"Not to worry," said Fred. "It's going to be a great show. Dr. Hairball is going to judge. He's Snuff's vet."

"How about the prizes?" asked Brother.

"That's the best part," said Fred. "Mr. Brown's company makes Arfo Dog Treats. Every dog will get a bag of Arfo Dog Treats. The grand prize will be a year's supply."

"Wow!" said Brother.

"Awesome!" said Sister.

Snuff looked sad when he heard Dr. Hairball's name.

But he danced for joy when he heard the words *Arfo Dog Treats*.

Snuff loved Arfo Dog Treats.

Fred watched Snuff dance. He got an idea.

"Hmm," he said. "Let's try those tricks again."

"Snuff, roll over!" said Fred.

Snuff rolled over.

"Snuff, shake hands!" said Fred.

Snuff shook hands.

"Snuff, sit up and beg!" said Fred.

Snuff sat up and begged.

"Good dog! Good dog!" said Fred.

Fred grabbed Snuff. They rolled around in the grass. Brother and Sister joined in.

Fred's mom came out on the front porch with a tray.

"Lemonade!" she cried.

"Lemonade!" shouted Fred, Brother, and Sister. Snuff barked.

They all raced to the front porch.

Snuff won.

If there was anything Snuff liked better than Arfo Dog Treats, it was lemonade.

Just up the road, Lizzy Bruin was working with Taffy, her collie. They were getting ready for the dog show, too. Lizzy was teaching Taffy to fetch. She picked up a stick and threw it.

"Taffy, go fetch!" she said.

But Taffy didn't go fetch. She just sat there.

"Please, Taffy," said Lizzy. "This is going to be your trick for the dog show. Let's try it again."

Lizzy picked up another stick and threw it.

"Taffy, go fetch!" said Lizzy.

But Taffy still didn't go fetch. She just sat there.

Lizzy's brother Buzz watched.

"I don't know what to do, Buzz," said Lizzy. "She doesn't seem to get it."

"I have an idea," said Buzz. "Let's *show* Taffy what to do. Pretend I'm a dog. Throw the stick and say 'Go fetch.'"

"Okay," said Lizzy. She picked up a stick and threw it. "Buzz, go fetch!" she said.

"Arf! Arf!" said Buzz. He raced
after the stick. He picked it up in his
mouth and came back with it.

Lizzy patted Buzz. "Good dog! Good dog!" she said.

"Now it's your turn, Taffy." She picked the stick up and threw it.

"Taffy, go fetch!" she said.

The stick sailed in the air. But Taffy didn't even watch it. She was fast asleep.

"What do you think?" said Lizzy.

"I think you better think of another trick," said Buzz.

Lizzy's dad was watching from the window.

"This dog show," he said to Lizzy's mom. "When is it?"

"Next Saturday," she said. "It's part of the church fair."

"I hope they can handle it," said Lizzy's dad.

"I'll be there," said Lizzy's mom. "I'll keep an eye on them."

Babs Bruno lived across the road from Lizzy. She liked to watch TV with her bulldog, Butch. Babs liked to watch cartoons. Butch liked to watch dog food ads.

One day, they saw a show they both liked.

It was a show about a dog. His name was Frisbee. He jumped up and caught Frisbees in his mouth.

"What a good trick!" said Babs.

"Butch," said Babs, "you can do

that in the dog show. But first we have to find my Frisbee."

They found it in the toy box.

"Look out, dog show!" said Babs. "Here we come!"

They went outside.

Babs threw the Frisbee. It was a good throw. The Frisbee sailed on the air.

Butch raced after it. He leaped in the air. He caught the Frisbee in his mouth.

Then he got it on the ground and chewed it to pieces.

"That was pretty good," said Babs. "Except for the last part."

A police car stopped in front of Babs's house. The chief got out. He was reading something.

"Hi, Dad," said Babs. "What are you reading?"

"I'm reading about the church fair," said Chief Bruno. "It's going to be something. There's a bake sale. There's a clothing sale. There's an attic sale. And look at this. There's going to be a dog show. Have you heard about it?"

"Heard about it?" said Babs. "Butch and I are getting ready for it."

Chief Bruno looked at the chewed Frisbee.

"Uh-huh," said the chief.

He went into the house. Inside, he tripped.

"What's all this junk?" he said.

"That's not junk," said Mrs. Bruno. "Those are things for the attic sale."

"Yes, of course," said the chief.

He knew about the attic sale.

He knew about the bake sale and the old-clothes sale.

But the dog show was something new. It worried him.

Officer Marguerite would be on duty next Saturday. She'd keep an eye on things.

5

Dogs and dog owners all over town were getting ready for the big show.

Queenie McBear had a dog. His name was Hot Dog. Queenie tried to teach Hot Dog to walk on his hind legs. Hot Dog had a long body and short legs. It was hard for him to walk on his hind legs. He got tired of trying.

He lay down and rolled over.

Hot Dog was very good at it.

"That's it!" said Queenie. "Your trick can be rolling over."

"Woof!" said Hot Dog.

"Hot Dog, roll over," she said.

Hot Dog rolled over—and over and over and over.

"Good dog!" said Queenie.

Billy Bearson had a poodle.

Her name was Fifi.

He was training Fifi to wear a collar and leash. Fifi didn't like them.

Billy put them on. Fifi twisted and turned and got them off.

"Please, Fifi," said Billy. "You have to have a collar and a leash. It's the rules."

Billy put them on, and Fifi took them off.

Billy got an idea. That could be Fifi's trick.

She would be an escape artist.

Billy put them on again.

"Escape, Fifi, escape!" said Billy.

Fifi escaped.

"Good dog!" said Billy.

Annie Dobbs had a Scottie.

His name was Scottie. Annie loved Scottie. She wanted him to be in the dog show.

Scottie knew some good tricks.

He could catch a ball.

He could jump over a low fence.

But he had a bad habit. When he

got excited, he chased his tail. He chased it until he got dizzy and fell down.

Annie tried to get him to catch a ball.

But he got excited.

He chased his tail until he got dizzy and fell down.

Then she tried to get him to jump over a fence. The same thing happened.

Annie got an idea. *That* would be Scottie's trick.

"Spin, Scottie, spin!" said Annie.

Scottie spun. He spun until he got dizzy and fell down.

"Good dog!" said Annie.

Sam McNab needed a trick for his big sheepdog, Cuddles.

He tried to teach him to fetch.

But Cuddles didn't want to.

He tried to teach him to catch a ball.

But Cuddles didn't want to.

He tried to teach him to go through a hoop.

But Cuddles didn't want to.

The only thing Cuddles wanted to do was herd sheep. But there were no sheep for Cuddles to herd.

Cuddles kept nudging Sam the whole time. Pushing and nudging, nudging and pushing.

Sam got mad.

"What do you think you're doing, Cuddles?" said Sam.

Then Sam figured out what Cuddles thought he was doing. *He was herding Sam!*

"That will be your trick!" said Sam. "I'll say 'Ba-a-a-a,' and you'll herd me."

Sam said, "Ba-a-a-a!" Cuddles herded him right off his feet.

Sam reached up and scratched Cuddles under the chin.

"Good dog!" he said.

Lady Grizzly heard about the show.

"Greeves," she said, "I wish to enter Yasha and Sasha."

"Yes, ma'am," said Greeves. "They say the dogs must do some sort of trick. What do you think they should do?"

Yasha and Sasha lay at Lady Grizzly's feet. Their tongues were hanging out. Yasha's tongue was as long as a small dog. Sasha's was even longer.

"Hmm, what should they do?" said Lady Grizzly. "*Anything they want to*. That's what!"

6

There was a lot of excitement about
the fair.

Even Minister Jones was excited.
He took down the sign on the gate.
He put up a bigger and better one.
This is what it looked like.

Folks stopped and looked at the sign.

"Look!" said one. "They're adding a dog show this year!"

"And look!" said another. "A prize for each and every dog!"

"I've got six dogs," said another. "I'm going to enter them all!"

Meanwhile, the Bears' tree house was filling up with all kinds of cakes and pies. There were chocolate cakes, angel food cakes, and pound cakes. There were apple pies, cherry pies, and banana cream pies.

Cousin Fred's house was full of old clothes: old coats, old hats, old shirts, old pants, old everything.

Babs Bruno's house was full of enough stuff to fill a junkyard.

But Mama wasn't worried about the bake sale or the other sales. She was worried about the dog show.

"Papa, I'm worried about the dog show," she said. "I think the cubs may have bitten off more than they can chew. Putting on a show of *any* kind is a big job. But a dog show . . ."

"Not to worry," said Papa. "We'll be there to keep an eye on things. Fred's mom is in charge of the clothing sale. She'll keep an eye on things. Mrs. Bruno is in charge of the attic sale. She'll keep an eye on things. Minister Jones is in charge of the whole fair. He'll *surely* keep an eye on things.

"So, as I say: *not to worry!* With all of us keeping an eye on things, what could *possibly* go wrong?"

"I suppose you're right," said Mama.

But she still worried.

It was Friday. It was the day before the fair.

There was still a lot to do.

The stage for the dog show still had to be built.

The baked goods had to be taken to the fair.

The clothing had to be taken to the fair.

The attic stuff had to be taken to the fair.

Folding chairs had to be carried up from the church basement.

The sales tables had to be set up.

But it all got done!

Finally, it was Saturday! It was the day of the fair!

The day dawned bright and sunny.

There was a breeze.

It blew the leaves.

It blew the bushes.

The breeze got stronger.

It blew a poster hanging on a tree.

It was a poster for the dog show.

The poster came loose.

It sailed high in the air. It twisted and turned in the breeze.

It sailed over the Bears' tree house. The Bear family was having breakfast. If they had looked out the window, they might have seen it.

But they didn't. They were too busy talking about their plans for the day.

It sailed over Cousin Fred's.

Snuff had learned to shake hands and sit up.

It sailed over Lizzy Bruin's.

Taffy had learned to go fetch.

It sailed over Babs Bruno's.

Butch was still chewing the Frisbee to pieces. But that was okay. Babs had gotten some extra Frisbees.

JUNKYARD

It sailed over the churchyard.

Minister Jones was putting out the clothes and the attic treasures. The baked goods wouldn't go out until the last minute.

It sailed over the police station.

Chief Bruno was already at work. He was still worried about the dog show. He told Officer Marguerite to keep an eye on things. *Again.*

It sailed over the Arfo Dog Treats factory.

Far, far below, the big Arfo truck was loading up.

It sailed higher and higher.

It joined a flock of geese flying north.

It parted ways with the geese.

It began to come down.

It sailed low along Junkyard Road.

It almost came down in the junkyard.

But a fresh breeze picked it up and sent it sailing again.

It sailed into the woods behind the junkyard.

There was a clubhouse in the woods behind the junkyard. It was the secret clubhouse of the Too-Tall gang.

It was made out of old car and truck parts that the gang had taken from the junkyard.

Too-Tall was the head of the gang. He sat on a big truck seat. It was almost like a throne.

Skuzz, Vinnie, and Smirk sat on an old car seat.

The Too-Tall gang was a nasty bunch.

During school, it was easy for them to find nasty things to do. They could beat up first graders. They could throw girls' hats into the trees. They could put worms down girls' backs.

But with school out, it wasn't easy finding nasty things to do.

There was an old-time car horn on the arm of Too-Tall's truck seat. It was the kind of horn that went *HONK*. Too-Tall punched it hard. It went *HONK*.

"This meeting will come to order!" he said. "Or else!"

The meeting came to order.

"The floor is open for ideas," said Too-Tall. "And they *better* be good!"

"Er, how about if we knock over some trash cans?" said Skuzz.

"Na-a-a-a-a-h," said Too-Tall. "Knockin' over trash cans is old stuff. Besides, it's not trash day."

"I've been lookin' around," said Vinnie. "I see that Farmer Ben has a new scarecrow. It's pretty nice. It's got a scarf and a top hat. Let's knock *it* over. I wouldn't mind havin' that top hat."

"Maybe," said Too-Tall. "But it might be a trap. Farmer Ben's still mad about the last scarecrow we knocked over."

"We could raid Ben's apple trees," said Smirk.

"Nope," said Too-Tall. "Ben's apples are still green."

"We could catch some frogs and turn 'em loose in the library," said Skuzz.

"Not bad," said Too-Tall. "But the frog pond is two miles away."

Was it possible that the nasty Too-Tall gang was stuck?

It was a good thing the clubhouse window was open. Or else the gang might have been stuck all day.

At that very moment, the dog-show poster sailed through the window. It dropped to the floor.

Skuzz picked it up.

"Hey, lookit," he said. "They're having some kind of dog show at the church fair."

"Gimme that," said Too-Tall. He took hold of the poster.

"Hmm," said Too-Tall. "A dog show this afternoon. Great. That gives us plenty of time."

"Plenty of time for what?" asked Skuzz.

"Plenty of time to crash the dog show," said Too-Tall.

"I heard of crashin' parties," said Vinnie. "But how do you crash a dog show?"

"Easy," said Too-Tall.

He got up from his throne. He

pulled the gang in close and told them his plan.

"Cats?" said Smirk. "Where are we gonna get cats?"

"At the junkyard," said Too-Tall.

"Yeah!" said Skuzz. "Junkyard cats!"

"The meanest, nastiest cats ever," said Vinnie.

"Cats after our own hearts," said Smirk.

The gang stole through the woods. They looked down Junkyard Road. They stole along the junkyard fence. Too-Tall was carrying a sack.

They came to the place where the fence was loose at the bottom.

They looked both ways. There was nobody in sight.

"Okay, Skuzz," said Too-Tall. "You lift the fence so we can get in. Then wait for us. Listen for a low whistle. Like this." Too-Tall whistled. "That will mean that we've got the cats. Then *you* whistle back when the coast is clear. Got it?"

Skuzz was scared.

"G-g-got it," he said. He lifted the fence. The gang crawled under.

Skuzz got more and more scared as he waited. What if somebody came along? What if Chief Bruno came along in the police car?

Skuzz looked through the fence.

There was no sign of the gang. He paced.

What was taking so long?

At last, there was a low whistle.

Skuzz made sure the coast was clear.

He started to whistle back.

But nothing happened!

His mouth had gone dry.

Another whistle from the junk-yard.

Skuzz started to whistle again. But still no whistle.

Too-Tall got tired of waiting.

He came charging out of the junkyard with the rest of the gang. He was carrying the sack. It was filled with hissing, spitting junkyard cats.

"Why didn't you whistle?" asked Too-Tall.

Skuzz pointed to his lips.

"Dry mouth," he said.

"So what?" Too-Tall said. "Now lift this fence and let us out of here. We've got a dog show to crash."

Officer Marguerite was keeping an eye on things. There wasn't much to keep an eye on yet. The fair wouldn't open until three o'clock.

She liked having church-fair duty. She had had it last year. She enjoyed it a lot.

She had gotten things at last year's bake sale.

She had gotten a scarf at the clothing sale.

She had gotten a clock at the attic sale.

The sales looked even better this year.

She saw a big red hat that she liked. There was a purple cape.

She held the cape up.

"What a lovely cape," she said.

"It *is* lovely," said Mama. "Why don't you buy it?"

Mama was bringing out the baked goods.

"Goodness," said Officer Marguerite. "What would I do with a purple cape?"

"Er, Officer Marguerite," said Mama.

"Yes?"

"The chief just drove up," said Mama. "I think he wants to talk to you."

Marguerite put down the purple cape.

She ran over to the chief's car.

The chief rolled down the window.

"How's it going?" he asked.

"All is calm," said Marguerite.

"It might be the calm before the storm," said Chief Bruno. "It's the dog show that worries me."

"Not to worry, Chief," said Marguerite. "What could *possibly* go wrong?"

The churchyard gates opened at three o'clock sharp. The crowd went in.

They licked their lips at the baked goods.

They went pawing through the clothing.

They tried on hats.

They tried on gowns.

They tried on the purple cape.

They oohed and aahed at the attic treasures.

They tried out bent golf clubs.

They looked through broken telescopes.

They sat on chairs with no bottoms.

The dog show drew the biggest crowd. Every seat was filled. There was a long line of dogs and dog owners.

The huge Arfo truck stopped in front of the church. There was a picture of a bag of Arfo Dog Treats on the side.

"Arf!" said Snuff when he saw it. He did his little dance.

"Down, boy!" said Fred.

The dogs were ready.

The dog owners were ready.

The Too-Tall gang was also ready. They had sneaked up behind the church. They had sneaked into the churchyard. Now they were hidden behind the stage on which Minister Jones was standing.

"Welcome," said Minister Jones. "Welcome to the first dog show ever. I shall now turn you over to Dr. Hairball, the judge."

Dr. Hairball climbed onto the stage.

He raised his arms and said . . .

"Let the grand parade of dogs begin!"

With Fred and Snuff in the lead, the grand parade began.

And that's when Too-Tall let the cats out of the bag.

There was a split second of silence. The cats and the dogs looked at each other.

Then hisses, screeches, snarls, yelps, and howls broke out.

Junkyard cats are mean. But there was an army of yapping, barking, yowling dogs. There were just a few junkyard cats.

The Too-Tall gang was pleased.

They had crashed the dog show. And they had turned the church fair into a war zone.

Dogs were chasing cats every which way.

They chased them through the bake sale. Tables were turned over. Cakes and pies flew through the air.

Folks were slipping and sliding on whipped cream and icing.

A banana cream pie hit Dr. Hairball full in the face.

An angel food cake landed on Minister Jones's head.

Yasha and Sasha dragged Greeves through the clothing sale.

Yasha came out wearing the big red hat.

Sasha came out wearing the purple cape.

Greeves tried to hold on. But he got left behind in a pile of old clothes.

Snuff pulled at his leash.

"Sit!" cried Fred.

But Snuff pulled free and was gone.

Butch and Cuddles chased some cats through the attic sale. Things flew through the air. Vases and lamps bonked folks on the head.

Dogs and cats were running amuck.

Officer Marguerite reached for her cell phone. She called Chief Bruno. She called the fire chief. She called the dogcatcher.

There was a tree in the corner of the churchyard. The cats climbed the tree. Dogs pawed and barked and yelped at the foot of the tree.

Cubs and grownups shouted and screamed.

Fred was worried. He couldn't find Snuff.

"I can't find Snuff!" he cried.

"I think I see him!" shouted Brother.

"He's over there beside the truck!" yelled Sister.

Snuff hadn't chased the cats. He was staring at the picture of the Arfo Dog Treats bag on the side of the truck.

The Too-Tall gang saw him, too.

It gave them an idea.

They sneaked over to the truck.

They let down the gate.

They climbed into the truck.

They threw down the bags. The bags broke open. Arfo Dog Treats poured out.

Snuff went nuts. He gobbled them down.

Yasha and Sasha saw the dog treats. So did the other dogs. They forgot about the cats. They went after the dog treats.

Yasha and Sasha climbed into the truck. They tore open more bags. Dog treats poured out of the truck.

The dogs all climbed into the truck. They went after the treats. The Too-Tall gang got scared. They jumped out of the truck. They climbed the tree.

The dogs ate their fill of Arfo Dog Treats.

More than their fill.

Chief Bruno came. The siren was screaming.

The fire chief came in a cherry picker.

The dogcatcher came with a big net.

They got the cats out of the tree.

They turned them loose.

They got the Too-Tall gang down, too. But they didn't turn *them* loose. Chief Bruno made them sit in the police car.

In the end, they didn't need the dogcatcher. The dogs had eaten so many dog treats that they could hardly move.

The dogs didn't get to do their tricks.

Except for pooping all over the place!

But each and every dog did get a prize: all the dog treats they had eaten.

Each dog and owner also got a certificate.

This is what it looked like:

CERTIFICATE

This is to certify that

(DOG'S NAME) _

and

(DOG'S OWNER'S
   NAME) _

participated in the first
(and last)
Church Fair Dog Show —
which will be known forever as

The Great Runamuck
Dog Show!

Minister Jones and all the others who worked so hard on the church fair had a meeting.

What should they do?

Should they cancel the fair or put it off?

They decided to put it off.

They would go to work and put the fair on in two weeks.

Without a dog show, of course.

But there was one problem.

It was a big problem.

The churchyard was a terrible, awful, rotten (and smelly) mess.

Chief Bruno solved the problem.

He gave the gang a choice:

They could go before Judge Gavel.

Or they could change their name to the Pooper-Scooper Cleanup gang and clean up the whole terrible, awful, rotten (and smelly) mess.

It was a big job.

A *very* big job.

But the churchyard was fresh and clean when the fair was held two weeks later.

Without a dog show, of course.

As for Arfo Dog Treats . . .

Poor Snuff was never able to look at another Arfo Dog Treat ever again.

Don't miss the next
Berenstain Bears
Stepping Stone Book™:
THE WRONG
CROWD

HERE IS AN EXCERPT.

So far, it had been a fun summer.

On most days, Sister went to the playground with her best friend, Lizzy Bruin.

They ran around the track.

They pushed each other on the swings.

They jumped rope. There was always a third for double Dutch.

There was another good thing about the playground.

Teacher Jane was in charge. Teacher Jane was Sister's teacher. Watching the playground was her summer job.

There wasn't a lot of trouble at the playground. But there was *some*.

It was mostly caused by Too-Tall and his gang.

They pushed and shoved.

They picked on younger cubs.

They did all the mean things bullies do.

Then one day, Too-Tall snatched Sister's best hair bow from her head.

Sister tried to grab it back.

But Too-Tall was too tall!

Sister screamed and shouted. "Give me back my hair bow, you big bully!"

Too-Tall laughed down at her.

Then he threw Sister's best hair bow up into a tree.

Sister screamed some more.

That was when Brother came along.

He had been playing basketball with Cousin Fred. Brother marched up to Too-Tall.

He stood toe to toe with Too-Tall. His nose came up to Too-Tall's chest.

Too-Tall really *was* tall.

Stan and Jan have been writing and illustrating books about the Berenstain Bears for many years. They live on a hillside in Bucks County, Pennsylvania, a place that looks a lot like Bear Country. They see deer, wild turkeys, rabbits, squirrels, and woodchucks through their studio window almost every day—but no bears. The Bears live inside their hearts and minds.

Stan and Jan have two sons. Their names are Michael and Leo. Leo is a writer. Michael is an illustrator. They help their parents write and illustrate the books. Stan and Jan have four grandchildren. One of them can already draw pretty good bears.